In the Backrooms

A survivor's story

by Bonissi Matteo

Front cover picture by: Alexandr Ivanov (Pexels.com)
Rear cover picture by: Oleg Magni (Pexels.com)

First Edition

I do believe they exist.
And, if they really do, pray that you are lucky enough to never fall there.

Introduction

I heard the door ring.

My receptionist pushed the button to open the door.

I stopped looking at the closed entrance of my office and moved my eyes towards a man, who was taking his coat and his hat.

<< So, the next appointment is in two weeks? >> he asked.

<< That is correct >>

<< Thank you, for today >>

I slowly opened my arms and raised my shoulders.

<< That's what my job is supposed to be >> I answered, smiling.

He replied the smile, told me goodbye and left.

I turned around, walking towards my desk.

Taking up my water bottle, I started looking at my agenda, which laid open on the table.

H: 15:00 – 16:15. Mr. John McSimon. Paranoia, trouble sleeping, PTSD (?).

I gazed at the clock.

Mr. Garfield, who had just left my office, was strangely fast today.

Usually, he finished late.

Not this time.

Maybe he's really improving I thought, as I took a sip from my bottle.

It was May, and outside it was raining.

The sky was covered in a thick layer of clouds, yet in the distance, I was able to see some light beams penetrating the grey formations.

As I took another sip, I looked again at the time.

14:53.

Putting down the bottle, I pressed the button that advised my secretary to let the next patient enter.

After a couple of seconds, I saw the doorknob rotate.

Alice's voice told a stranger that he could go inside.

I smiled.

It was a new patient.

And, since he was new, I was aware that I had to give him the best first impression possible.

<< Mr. McSimon, pleased to meet you >>

<< G'day sir >> he replied, with an unsure voice.

It was very low.

He was very probably intimidated.

Not by me, physically.

Yet, most of my patients had a similar behavior the first time they came here.

Some, not only the first time.

<< Please, feel like at home... first time? >>

<< What? Oh, no no >>

He smiled, with an expression that was half sadness and half embarrassment.

<< I am aware that I have to lay down there and tell you what happened >>

<< Yes, that is the first step in therapy, can I use this word with you right? >>

He nodded a yes.

<< Great, then we can analyze together what happened and how I could try to help you >>

He was nervous, and I could tell this by the fact that he was biting his own lower lip.

He sat down.

And I did the same.

An awkward silence fell into the room.

CHAPTER I: THE ACCIDENT

<< Okay >>

He broke the silence.

Finally.

He had been sitting there without saying anything for a couple of minutes now, and I was getting ready to ask the first question.

Usually, I prefer having them talk to me.

It is more natural.

Especially the first time.

<< I think I should start from the beginning >>

<< Yes, if you do believe it could help me understand the accident, or whatever you described with that word >>

<< The fall >>

<< The fall? >>

<< Yes, I fell there >>

He took a deep breath, and he started telling me what had happened.

It was last November, and he was walking home after having visited a friend.

As he was crossing an empty street, he fell.

Yet, when he got up, he noticed that something was off.

He was not in Chicago anymore.

Nor, he was outside.

Truth be told, he was in someplace that he swore had already visited before.

Maybe in a dream.

As he started to describe the place, I could see his eyes widen.

His left foot started to move.

Rapidly.

Almost unnoticed.

He got up in an empty room.

It was yellow.

But not the same color that children use to draw the sun in the corner of a page.

It was more like… piss-yellow.

That was the word he used.

The room had no door.

He rubbed his eyes, and when he opened them, nothing had changed.

He then noticed that his hands were wet.

By looking around, he saw a small line of water following the wall behind him down.

And around him, the carpet was wet.

He cleaned his hands on his jacket, thinking that he had just landed in a pool of piss.

He sniffed a finger and was happy to find out that the fluid was, in fact, not urine.

Yet, he felt unsure if he wanted to taste it, as its odor was similar to what he described as copper.

<< I slapped myself in the face >>

<< Why? >>

<< I… I thought that I was dreaming or, I don't know, on some kind of trip >>

<< Had you been using drugs that day or the days prior? >>

<< No, I'm clean. I used to do coke some years ago, but it was only because the work turns were inhumane. When I left, I stopped >>

Yet, he wasn't dreaming.

He started to move towards what seemed like the place a door should have been present.

Slowly, he looked over the side of the wall.

He saw a similar room.

Again.

And again.

And another time.

It was as if the room was repeating itself.

He couldn't believe it.

He slapped himself again, this time harder.

But nothing had changed.

He went forward.

Maybe, he reasoned, he could find the exit where it seemed that the weird "room-corridor" was ending.

As he was moving, he found out that the carpet on which he was walking over was wet everywhere.

With at least an eighth of a foot, he stated.

<< Of a foot? >>

<< No, sorry, an eighth of an inch, my bad >>

<< Oh okay, that's a little, you know, less wet >> I joked.

He was stressed.

I could surely tell that.

I hoped that by joking he could relieve some of his negative energy.

But I failed.

He did not notice my joke, or he did and decided to move on.

Still, he continued with his story.

He described the smell.

Horrible.

As if the person who created that room wanted to make you puke.

At least, the temperature was normal.

Outside, that day had been freezing.

But here, he was able to open his coat and loosen his scarf.

He reached the end of the corridor.

On his right, there was a wall.

Therefore, he turned to his left.

And he stood there, in shock.

He was shocked about what was there.

And, what wasn't.

Another similar room.

And, behind, another one.

There was nothing else.

Room after room.

He started moving faster.

But still, wherever he went, he was still in that sort of weird piss-looking place.

At first, he walked faster.

Then, he ran.

For around fifteen minutes, he ran.

Non-stop.

<< It was weird, I've never run that much in my life, and I wasn't tired >>

He told me he was starting to think that he had gone insane.

He then stopped.

He sat down for a minute or two.

Not because he had to catch his breath.

Just, to try and understand what was happening.

As he sat, he tried to use his senses to help him.

He concentrated.

His sight.

He knew he was in some kind of maze, a very big one.

Maybe it was real, or maybe it wasn't.

Maybe he was dead, but couldn't find it out by himself.

He started to hate the piss-yellow.

And the lack of furniture in the rooms.

His smell.

Terrible.

Copper-like wet.

He was almost sure there were also some parts of the rooms that smelled of urine, but he reckoned that maybe it was his mind playing a trick on him.

His touch.

The carpet was wet.

With a substance of unknown origin that didn't look safe to drink.

Not that he was thirsty.

Just, he didn't want to risk it.

Also because he hadn't seen a toiler around.

Maybe that could explain the weird odor of the room, maybe it was rotten feces.

He tried not to think about that idea.

His taste.

Heck no.

He did not want to taste anything.

Not by any chance.

Still, he was sure that he wasn't hungry.

Nor thirsty.

Despite not having eaten that much on that day.

He tried looking into his pocket, searching for his watch.

Sadly for him, there was no trace of it.

He was sure he had it in his pocket before.

Its wristband was damaged, so not to lose it, he kept it in a pocket of his jacket.

But there was no trace of it.

Maybe it fell when he entered that weird place.

Or maybe he left it at his friend's house.

He hoped for the latter.

It was his favorite watch.

His hearing.

Now that he focused on it, he noticed something.

A buzzing sound.

It was monotonous, with some very small variations.
He quickly found where it came from.
The lights.
Those were the producers of that sound.
The humming from the lighting system was very low.
But it was the only sound he could hear.
And so it felt as if its volume was ten times higher.
Or maybe even more.
As he was scanning his surroundings with his ears, he
noticed something.
Another sound.
Very different from the buzzing one.
It was more... << Alive >>
<< Alive? Like, a person? >>
<< Don't know >>
<< You didn't go and try to see who was making that
noise? >>
<< Heck no >>
<< Why not? >>
<< Because I felt as if I was being watched. Maybe by
humans, maybe by animals. And I was sure that, if I
could hear that thing, the chances of it hearing me were
very high. I mean, it felt as if those rooms had been
there for decades, and I was new there. But my guts,
they told me that the thing out there was more expert
of that place than I was >>
<< So, what... you... >>
<< What I did? >>

<< Yeah >>

<< I got T. F. away >>

I looked him in his eyes.

I raised his shoulders and continued.

<< I am no genius man. But I am clever enough to know when some situation is dangerous. And that place, it felt like, I don't know, death >>

<< You felt in danger? >>

<< Yes, but not in a violent way. It was not like a clown tent or a killer's house. It was more in a "forgotten" way, you know? >>

<< What do you mean? >>

<< I was afraid of getting lost there. I already was. But I wasn't keen on remaining there. I had to come out of that place. I had to come back "here" >> he replied, pointing his fingers to the ground.

<< I see >>

I finished writing down a note in my small book.

As a psychologist, I was used to writing notes fast.

I was recording the session too.

My patients know that, of course.

It is written on my website, on the office door, and in the "contract" they sign for every session.

I use the recordings to listen to the patient again and again when I need to find what they are thinking at.

Yet, I still try to take all my notes in one go.

<< So, you started walking away from what you thought was the location of the sound? >>

<< Walking? No, I ran >>

<< Weren't you scared that the person or animal could hear you running, and run after you? >>

<< Yes, but I didn't think about that at that moment, I was too busy trying to put as much distance as humanly possible between me and it >>

<< And how did it go? >>

Horrible.

He went into a section that was moister on the pavement compared to the previous ones.

That meant that, of course, each step was joined by a splashing sound.

And that thing surely heard the noise.

I looked at the clock.

Not that I was too annoyed with the story.

Quite the opposite, I found it interesting.

It's just that he had started describing in a technical way the rooms he was running into.

And those were all the same.

Sometimes, he would stop for a second, during which I would take the chance to drink a little.

I offered him something to drink, but he refused.

He then completely stopped talking.

We exchanged eye contact.

His expression, I couldn't understand.

He put his hands over his head and turned it down.

I asked him if he was alright, and he told me that he was.

Of course, that was false.

If he had been alright, he wouldn't have been in my office.

He was struggling with something.

I could see it.

He then took a deep breath and continued.

<< I then turned into a dead-end corner >> he stated.

I slightly changed my position on my chair.

<< And what happened next? >>

He told me that he couldn't go forward.

He was stuck.

He thought he was done for.

He could hear the animal getting closer and closer.

He could hear the steps on the moist.

Splash.

He had no chance to escape.

Splash.

It was near.

Splash.

He went to the end of the corridor and placed his back on the wall.

He wanted to face the beast face to face.

Silence had fallen on that place.

Even the buzzing noise of the lights seemed to fade down.

Maybe, it was a prank.

He hoped.

He prayed for that to be the case.

A prank of a sick-minded person.
Otherwise, he would have been done for.
He had no girlfriend, yet he would have been surely missed by his parents.
Maybe, they would have sought after him.
Maybe, he hoped, they would arrive in seconds and scare the beast away.
That would have been potentially his last chance of escape.
They could have killed the animal.
Or, scared it.
Or even distracted it.
What if the search party would also become lost here as well?
They would have surely been doomed too.
Or maybe they knew how to escape.
The splashes were very near.
The beast was around the corner.
He pressed his back on the wall.
Maybe, if he stayed still, he would not be seen.
He had no weapon.
The most similar thing to a knife that he had with him, were his house keys.
He grabbed them.
Keeping them very tight in his fist.
And close to his body.
He was ready, he thought.
Not ready to win.

Yet, he hoped to at least be able to injure the beast.
Maybe, it would stop it from harassing other lost people.
He would sacrifice himself for unknown others.
As he was thinking about this, he noticed something moving.
Near the corner of the wall.
A shadow.
Getting bigger.
And more defined.
Definitely, getting nearer.
He was sure that potentially his underwear could soon become wet.
Then, he saw it.

It was as nothing he had ever seen.
It surely wasn't human.
But it wasn't an animal either.
At least, not a dog.
Nor a wolf or a bear.
It was as if a tree had been separated by its leaves and the trunk and branches had been painted completely pitch black.
Where he thought the face was, no identifiable features could be found.
No eyes.
No hair.
No lips, mouth, nose, or chin.
It was literally like a broken branch.

The fact that it was so inhumane scared him to the bone.

It sent shivers down his spine.

The "dark tree" was not like anything he had ever seen.

Not even the most wicked and corrupted horror book had something as scary as that thing.

It was as if the entire universe had condensated all its negative feelings into a living being.

And that being was getting closer to him.

At first, he tried to remain still.

But the beast was still coming forward.

He then abandoned that strategy.

He wanted to defend himself.

But his hands were planning something else.

At first, he was able to keep his hands forward, as to put his keys between him and that thing.

But as the beast drew closer and closer, he felt as if it was overpowering him.

He felt negative energy around him.

He described it as a sensation of doom.

Hopelessness.

Defeat.

The beast was near.

Only a couple of yards separated the two.

He was shivering.

It was impassible.

The legs of the beast pushed forward.

Another step.

It was standing on two "branches".
And it had five "arms", other than the head.
Two on the left side.
Three on the right one.
One of the branches on the right side went slightly backward.
He knew it was going to strike soon.
It felt so natural.
Like when a runner pushed against the pavement to move forward.
Like when a jumper bends his or her knees to propel himself or herself higher.
That being, was preparing to strike.
John wanted to strike first.
Maybe a preemptive strike could have saved him, he remembered thinking.
But his body had other plans in mind.
As the beast started to move its arm forward, he covered his face with his arms.
A blinding light engulfed him.
What was before a being of darkness, it was as if had become the sun on Earth.
He couldn't see it.
It was covered by his arms.
Yet, he saw the light illuminating the scene.
And the slightly burning sensation of heat.
He thought that he had died.
It was the only logical solution.

Apparently, however, that solution was wrong.
He was still alive.
As the light started to turn down, and the heat
dissipated, he lowered his arms.
Maybe, he could strike now.
Yet, as he moved quickly to shove his keys into the
beast...

It wasn't there anymore.
John cautiously looked around.
He turned his head back, but nothing other than the wall
was behind him.
It had vanished.
In thin air.
As if...
As if it never existed!
It wasn't possible.
It was there.
Just seconds ago.
He started to panic.
Maybe it was its strategy.
Maybe it was waiting around the corner.
Luring him to come forward.
And then strike him.
So he stayed there.
Still.
Not moving.
Waiting.

For a sound.

For a shadow.

For anything.

Nothing.

Time passed.

And he remained there.

For what seemed like an eternity.

He grabbed what little courage he could.

And he did a step forward.

Still, silence.

Other than the splash of his foot.

And the buzzing noise.

Nothing.

He did another step.

And gradually he moved forward.

It took him probably a couple of minutes to reach the nearest part of the corridor.

There, he stopped.

Just before it.

He took a deep breath.

And slowly, started moving laterally.

He wanted to peak from the corner.

Yet, he was sure that he would find the beast on the other side.

Waiting for him.

Potentially, just mere inches from his face.

Yet, he had to try.

It wasn't as if he could stay there forever.
He wanted to find a way home.
He had to.
Unless he wanted to remain there.
In eternity.
Without almost even noticing it, he moved forward.
And he looked over the corner.
Nothing.
Only the room.
A light source was flickering above.
It created a small disturbance in the ambient noise.
But nothing else.
It was like before.
Nothing.
Only piss-yellow.

Making as less noise as possible, he went forward.
After another corner, still nothing.
No sign of that creature.
Slowly, he started to pick up his pace.
He then began to walk at normal speed.
He was on edge, trying to hear any possible sound.
He was scared of every corner, as that thing could be somewhere.
It had to be somewhere.
And like that, he went on and on.
No signs of the beast whatsoever.
He was starting to become paranoid.

His walk quickly became a fast jog.
Then he started running.
Where was that beast?
That was the only question in his mind.
He wanted to scream.
Attract that unearthly demon.
To fight it or die.
But he didn't scream.
He had no chance.
As, by accident, he tripped.
On his own feet.
He was sure he would have beaten his head against a wall.
So he closed his eyes.

CHAPTER II: DEEPER

When he opened them, he was somewhere else. At first, he was relieved of not being on that horrible carpet anymore.

It is cold.

Concrete.

The floor is made of wet concrete.

John looks around.

No more identical rooms.

He is in what appears to be an abandoned underground parking lot.

He started walking forward.

Slowly.

The good thing is that his steps are silent now.

No more splashes on the carpet.

He then remembered why he was running.

The beast.

He quickly looked behind him.

He moved so fast that he almost fell over.

Nothing.

Still complete emptiness.

That was good.

Yet, he was still scared.

The buzzing sound was still there.

Not as horrible as before.

A little bit less.

Still annoying.

Step after step, he went forward.

There were a lot of open doors and smaller corridors behind.

Some doors were closed, and he wasn't keen on opening them.

He was scared of what could potentially lay behind them.

Maybe the beast of before.

Or maybe something even scarier.

As he was looking around, he saw something within the corner of his eye.

He was on the right side of what could be described as a big corridor.

On the other side, around a hundred yards ahead, there was something.

Pushed by his curiosity, he got closer.

It was a box.

At first, he thought he was hallucinating.

It was the first piece of furniture, if the doors there were not counted, that he had encountered since he had entered the labyrinth,

He looked around.

Who could have placed it there?

It made no sense.

He then realized something even better.

It was not only a single box.

There were three of those.

In the middle of what was otherwise nothing.

Those were simple metal boxes.

Yet, something was strange about them.

He thought that the weirdness was potentially the fact that those were there for no apparent reason.

He approached the closest one.

He was tempted to open it.

Then he remembered.

Maybe this was a trap.

Maybe something was inside.

A creature perhaps.

Or a bomb.

Or something else equally dangerous.

He stood there, for a couple of minutes.

Staring at the handle that could be used to open it.

He slowly raised his hand.

It almost touched the handle, then stopped.

And stayed there for a minute.

In the meantime, his eyes were continuously going from the box, to his left, to his right, and then to the box again.

If something was going to happen, he wanted to know that as soon as possible.

He wasn't keen on being caught unprepared.

With the other hand, he held tight his keys.

A last look around.

What if someone owned them?

Could they be pissed off if he opened them?

If those were his, he would be.
He pushed his thoughts aside.
And touched the handle.
It was cold.
As much as the concrete floor.
He looked around.
Still nothing.
He took a deep breath and opened the lid.

He expected something.
A monster running toward him.
An explosion.
A spider.
Whatever, some sort of trap.
Nothing like that.
Inside, he found a flashlight, a bottle of water, and an energy bar.
He cautiously picked them up.
Still no trap.
He turned on the flashlight.
It worked.
That was great news.
While the place he was in was illuminated, there were still some dark spots.
And, somewhere in the distance, some lights often flickered.
In the worst-case scenario, he could still use the flashlight as a blunt object to protect himself.

The energy bar was not expired.
Another great news.
It was made with oatmeal and peanut butter.
He loved the former.
Sadly, he was allergic to the latter.
He rolled his eyes.
He hated his allergy.
Still, he placed both the torch and the energy bar in the pockets of his jacket.
He took a look at the water bottle.
It had a weird yellow label on it.
The color slightly remembered him of the rooms he was in before.
On the label, there was a woman.
But the interesting thing was the type of water, as this was no ordinary one.
Apparently, it was "almond water".
Something he had never tasted before.
He wasn't sure if he could trust it.
If it would be safe enough to drink.
And, if it was if his body would not throw it up later.
He opened it.
And he put his nose near the opening of the bottle.
It smelled actually good.
Maybe too good.
He was suspicious.
He decided to close the bottle and not drink it.
Even if he was slightly thirsty, he preferred to search for

normal water, not that weird one.

He looked around.

Still nothing, other than a never-ending corridor with hundreds if not thousands of doors.

So much space to explore.

To search for an exit.

He moved forward a little, to the next box.

Again, he slowly opened it.

No one could assure him that, having been lucky the first time, the second one could still be a trap.

Or the third one.

The second box was also interesting.

Inside, he found a couple of triple-A batteries, a small box of patches and, interestingly, a knife.

He took all the items inside.

The box of patches was immediately put in the left pocket of his trousers.

He wasn't injured, so he wasn't desperately needing those at the moment.

Yet they could become useful.

Hopefully, of course, those would not be needed.

The knife was small, but could also be useful.

He put that in his trousers as well.

He opened the torch and found that it ran on the same batteries as he had found.

Maybe, he wasn't so unlucky after all.

He quickly screwed back the end cap of the torch and

inserted in his pocket the spare batteries.
As he was going near the last box, he heard a sound.
A metallic one.
It was the sound of a light going off in the distance.
He turned towards the sound and, as expected, he saw
that far away one of the lights that illuminated the scene
had gone off.
Then, the next one.
And another one.
Slowly, he realized that the darkness was coming toward
him.
It scared him.
The lights turned off in rapid succession.
He froze in terror.
Something was off.
Maybe, it was his fault.
He knew he shouldn't have touched anything.
He was tempted to put the stuff back inside.
Or to run.
He did neither of those.
In a couple of seconds, he was into darkness.
Then, the lights came back on.

He saw something.
At least, the corner of his eyes did.
Slowly, terrified, he moved his head towards whatever
was attracting his view.
It was... a person?

He rubbed his eyes.

Yes, a person was there.

He got worried.

Maybe it was the owner of the boxes?

Or maybe, he was the technician who worked there and took care of the lights?

Maybe, he wasn't in the labyrinth anymore, but rather only in an almost abandoned place.

This comforted him.

Maybe, he could find a way home.

He looked behind himself, and seeing nothing, he faced the person.

<< Hey! >>

Nothing.

<< Hey you! >>

The person noticed him.

John waved.

The person waved back.

This put a smile on John.

He wasn't alone.

The other person had seen him.

He or she could maybe explain to him where he was.

Hopefully, even indicate him the way home.

Chicago is big, and maybe he was simply lost.

Maybe, he got hurt in the head and had regained consciousness in the parking lot of a hospital.

That was plausible.

He couldn't know all the parking lots in his city, he

thought.

The person was getting near.

It was potentially a woman, as it appeared to have long hair.

Yet, she was still too far for John to make up her facial expression.

He realized the stuff he had just put in his pocket could be hers.

He decided to probe the ground by admitting of having only some of the things he had found.

If those weren't hers, he could still keep them for himself.

Maybe even share them.

Or exchange the energy bar and the almond water for something that he could eat or drink.

That was a good idea.

<< Hey there, where are we? >>

The woman did not answer.

Weird.

She started gesticulating something.

Maybe she was blind.

<< You mean deaf, or mute? >> I asked him.

<< Yes, sorry, I meant mute, my bad >>

<< It's alright, go on >>

She could be mute.

Mute people exist.

And they are not worrisome at all.

John knew some mute and deaf people.

That woman, however, somehow scared him.

Something seemed off.

He reasoned that probably was just that he had been scared minutes before.

Maybe he was going crazy.

John still thought something about her was... absent.

He couldn't tell what, however.

Then, suddenly, some lights went off.

Some, in the distance.

And also those above the woman.

He could still see her figure in the dark, silhouetted against a lit background.

She was moving slowly.

But steadily.

As long as he could see her, he felt a little safer.

She was still getting closer.

She was a couple of dozen yards away.

The lights in the distance turned on.

Those nearby, over the female, did not.

It was weird, and he felt something in his stomach move.

He brushed it off as nothing.

The lights were still off.

And the woman was getting closer.

Now, he was starting to feel uneasy.

Then, the lights turned on.

He felt relieved.

She was close now.

And he wanted to see her face.
How she looked like.

<< What do you mean she had no face? >>
<< I swear, she didn't >>
<< But... >>
I closed my eyes, trying to visualize a person with no face.
It made no sense to me.
<< But I don't know how she could have been alive like that, I didn't stay there to ask! >>
<< You ran away? >>
<< You can bet I did! >>
<< I mean, it is reasonable, it's just that I don't understand! >>
<< Me neither, nor I could not care less. That thing was alive, it had no face and was coming towards me >>
He had started running away from the woman.
She still walked.
Apparently, she didn't try to pursue him.
He threw the energy bar at her.
Or, as to use the word he said, he *yeeted* it across the corridor and almost hit her.
She seemed a passive being.
Still, obviously, scary.
As he ran away, he turned toward her multiple times to keep an eye on her.
He also noticed that the boxes had disappeared.

While running, he touched his pockets to feel if he still had the stuff found with him.

He did.

So, he reasoned, those things were not a hallucination.

That was good news.

He wasn't going crazy.

Or at least, he hoped.

Ahead of him, he saw that the main corridor was in the shadow.

Sensing that those shadows could potentially hold something potentially dangerous, he decided to enter one of the open doors on the side.

He took a brief look at the woman with no face before he passed the door.

She was far away.

He was a little less worried now.

Maybe she had lost track of him.

Maybe she navigated with sound, and not with light.

He had not noticed any ears, but she had long black hair so he couldn't be sure.

Maybe she simply had a weird disease.

Maybe she wasn't hostile.

He still decided not to stick around to find out.

He went deeper into the corridor.

Passing some opened doors, he had to make some choices when he found a couple of crossways, and he followed his instincts.

While going around, he found two more boxes.

One, contained another set of batteries.

The other one was empty.

Maybe, he reasoned, someone else was around.

Hopefully, human.

And with a face.

Then, as he turned left at some point, he found himself in another big and long corridor like the one he was in before.

It wasn't the same, however, and this made him feel less agitated.

He was sure of this because, in this one, there was a building in a sort of opening.

It had some weird lights.

And people.

He slapped himself.

It wasn't a dream.

Maybe a hallucination.

But it seemed real.

He cautiously got closer.

His sight wasn't the best, yet he was sure that those people had a face.

With eyes, noses, and mouths.

And as he got near them, he could hear them talk.

At first, he was staying near the wall on one side, half-lit by the ceiling lights.

Then, he took courage and came forward into the light.

Into the center of the corridor.

Those were real people.

Maybe, he was close to getting out.

Maybe he was already out, yet he was suffering some side effects of some medications.

He had only one way to find out.

<< A diner? >>

<< Yeah, it's awkward to explain, but it was a real diner! In the middle of the corridor >>

Tom's Diner.

That was the name of the place.

It was quite big.

Around a couple of dozen people were there.

Most of them were grown-up adults.

There were also a couple of children.

He approached a man who was smoking a cigarette outside.

<< Hey, sir >>

<< Hello there >> the man answered.

John was relieved.

At least, that person could talk.

<< I think I got lost, may I ask where I am? >>

The man started to laugh.

John was a little offended, his question wasn't so out of place, he thought.

Turns out, he was wrong.

<< You really don't know where you are? >>

<< No... I mean, I know I might sound crazy, but I was in Chicago, I was walking and I fell and ended up in a

yellow room with a moisty carpet, I ran away from a black tree-like being and ended up here, where I had to run from a woman who had no face... I think I'm under some kind of drugs but I swear I'm not a drug addict... maybe it was some medications, I guess >>

<< From Chicago you say? >>

<< Yeah, in which part of the city are we? >>

<< We are in Level 1 >>

<< And, where is this place? >>

<< Oh, simple >> he smiled << In the backrooms >>

<< Ehm, where? >>

<< You never heard of the backrooms? >>

<< Is this some kind of neighborhood? >>

The man laughed again.

<< This is more than a single neighborhood, it is an entire universe >>

<< I don't understand >>

<< C'mon mate, I'll explain it to you. It will feel weird, but that's how it is >>

He then nodded to John to follow him inside.

<< Hey Tom, we've got a newbie here >>

A man with a chef outfit waved his right hand to John. And they sat down.

The man started to explain.

<< Wait, let me understand >> I tried to analyze what my patient had just told me << You are telling me that somewhere, potentially underneath us, there is a

parallel universe that can be entered by "falling"... >>

<< It's called "no-clipping" >>

<< Yes, that thing, and inside this universe, there are "levels", with "monsters" that try to kill you and... >>

I stopped for a second.

<< And no one told it to anyone? >>

<< That's the weird thing. Alex, the man who I met, told me that very few people are capable of coming back to reality, to the "front rooms", the place >> he indicated me and himself << where we both are >>

<< How? >>

<< I don't know, that's what Alex told me! >>

I write in my book: *Hallucinations, drugs? (maybe LSD?), Psychosis?*

He went on to explain this so-called "underworld".

He noted that the fact that it is under us is only speculation.

Simply by the fact that, to enter, you have to "no-clip" (i.e. fall) against a wall or the pavement.

John told me, that Alex informed him that the number of "levels" is undefined, and some of them are speculated as being as big as the Earth's surface itself.

CHAPTER III: UNDER US?

    I sat down on my couch.
My wife had just arrived home.
She gave me a kiss and went to take our children from school.
I looked over at my work suitcase.
I took my book.
Scrolling through the pages, I ended up on John's case.
I started reading what I had written after he left.

Mr. John McSimon – 1st Meeting.
Let's analyze what had happened to him until now, from when he entered to when he arrived at the diner.
At first, he was in the "front doors", the place where all of us normally live.
He then accidentally "no-clipped" as he fell down, and landed in the so-called "level zero", which is the place where most of those who enter end up.
The description of the physical appearance of the room was, apparently, shared by all those in the diner.
That place is "non-linear" and "liminal".
While I have never met this word before in my work, John described it as a "phase", a "transition" between one state (of matter and/or time) and another.
The "transition" that he described is potentially the one between usage and abandonment.
Alex told him about some other levels, and since he

(Alex) had met a lot of "travelers", he was able to also share with John a lot of their stories as well.

It appears that some of these "levels" resemble some "common abandoned place".

Level zero has been described similarly to the back rooms of an abandoned office.

The "backroomness" also gives the name to the universe, apparently.

Alex and others indicated that it is without "entities" (i.e. non-human beings?), while John and some stated of having seen or heard other potentially living beings in there.

John had an encounter of the third kind, and he wasn't the only one, yet his story was discredited by Alex as being a hallucination.

Having not met Alex (if he exists at all?), I could not confirm nor deny his solution to John's adventure.

It could have been a hallucination, or Alex was potentially "lucky" of having not met anything on level zero.

Then, there is level one.

The corridor with concrete walls and pavement.

Alex indicated it as an abandoned warehouse.

Here "sightings" and "encounters" have been indicated as "common".

Most of the creatures encountered are highly dangerous, apparently.

Also, John was very lucky of having met probably one of

the few "beings" that is passive.

It had been defined as a "faceling", a being with no face. Weird.

And creepy, but mainly weird.

John indicates the presence of other beings, such as lion-like predators, "smilers" (creepy night-loving entities who "smile"? and eat you), and "skin-eaters"(?).

I believe the patient suffers from heavy psychosis.

He briefly told me the story of the chef of the diner, Tom, who was a chef in the "front rooms" and decided to create a restaurant after he "no-clipped" (seriously?).

Some questions I hope of having answered in the next sessions, such as:

- Why do these people not try to leave?
- If they had tried, why had they not failed? (remember to ask John how he escaped!!!)
- Why do these creatures hunt humans and not other beings?
- How do "facelings" survive?
- Can he bring me any proof of the existence of this place?
- What is "almond water" and why is it important?

These questions I will try to answer hoping that the patient could express some "irregularities" (that would indicate his story as invented).

In the meantime, I need to know:

- Medical history, especially potential brain damage of the patient.

- Previous drug usages.
- Previous psychological history (hard!).

     As I sat there, reading my notes, I started wondering.
Why would someone fake something like this?
Is he a genius?
Has he suffered an accident?
If he's telling the truth… Nah, it can't be.

     I wanted answers.
And I knew I would soon obtain them, hopefully.
The next appointment had been scheduled for the following day.
I usually give the patients at least a week between each session.
But this time, it was different.
Maybe it was my "morbid" curiosity towards this weird place.
What if I fell there too?
That thought scared me that night.
And for the nights that followed.

<< Come in, please >>

<< G'day Doc >>

<< John, please to see you again and, please, call me Markus, let's be informal here >>

He took his time to get comfortable.

And then, he continued his story.

Alex and others in the diner tried to convince him to stay.

They reasoned that out there, he would be in danger, while the diner was safe.

If he wanted, they could have shown him some of the various "camps" of inhabitants of "level one".

He however decided to leave them.

Not because they were dangerous.

It's just that he wasn't like that.

They were basically people who had been "defeated" by that place.

Condemned to remain there for eternity.

Or, until death.

John wanted to try his luck.

He gathered some supplies, not without some difficulties, and went on his path.

After leaving the diner, he followed the big corridor in the opposite way that he had used before.

With that, he hoped, he would be able to avoid the facelings.

Even if those were peaceful (only the adult ones,

however), he still did not want to risk it.

He would avoid all entities if possible.

If not, he would fight them.

He went forward for what he stated as hours.

Endless corridors.

Doors.

Sometimes, stairs.

Yet, he avoided them.

Then, fed up with all the walking around, he decided to take a quick break.

He remained there for some minutes, eating a snack and drinking some almond water.

Alex had told him that it tasted great and had a sort of "cleansing effect" from the backroom-induced madness.

And he used a stair.

It was an ascending one.

Above him, the scenery was dark.

Yet, he used his torch to illuminate the area.

It looked similar to the place he was into.

The others at the diner had advised him to avoid stairs.

But still, he ascended them.

And found himself in a dark hallway.

Very narrow.

And wet.

He decided to turn back.

But when he turned, the stairs were gone.

He was scared to the bone.

He had just entered a zone that was specifically told to avoid: "level two".

That place was uncomfortable.
Unnerving.
Frightening.
Scary.
He hated it.
The pavement was soaking wet.
It did not look like water.
Not that he wanted to test if it was drinkable or not.
Along the walls, there were a lot of tubes.
Pipes.
Some of them were leaking, and that's where the liquid came from.
It was slightly slippery, yet he was able to remain standing.
The lighting was scarce.
So the corridor had huge chunks of darkness.
As he went forward, he noticed one thing.
It was getting hotter.
He had been advised of that.
He stopped for a second, to take off his jacket and place it into a backpack that he had obtained back at the diner.
And then he stopped talking.
I looked at him.
His hands were shaking.

I waited for some time.

As I was writing down what he had told me, I looked at him multiple times.

I stopped writing.

He looked at me.

His eyes were almost filled with tears.

Before I could say anything, he continued.

<< Then, I saw it >>

I placed the tip of my pencil on the paper.

I was ready to write down what he would have told me.

Or so I thought.

He told me that he had heard a sound behind him.

He turned.

In the distance, he saw a light.

In the tunnel.

And it was coming towards him.

Not fast, yet still noticeable.

He started walking fast in the opposite direction.

The light was gaining ground.

He started running.

He was making a lot of noise.

It did not matter.

He did not want to get caught by that thing.

<< What did it look like? >> I asked.

<< A smile >>

<< What? >>

<< A smiling face made of light over a black shadow >>

I raised my eyebrows.

A << Holy crap >> accidentally exited my mouth.

<< Yeah, and that thing was coming for me. I... I ran as fast as I could, I hated it, I still see it in my dreams, and I cannot get that damn thing out of my mind >>

He noticed that I was just slightly surprised.

Probably, he thought that my answer was fake.

So he took a piece of paper.

And drew that thing.

A "Smiler".

That's how he called that.

I gazed at it.

Just by looking, I felt goosebumps all over my body.

I wanted to tell him to get that nightmare off my face.

But he was my patient.

And I was the one that should be curing him.

Not hate the man who seeks my help.

I remained calm and impassible.

I will only describe it in one word.

AVOID.

At all costs.

He ran.

Fast.

That thing was still closing in.

He turned to the right.

It was a dead end.

He felt dying inside.

Yet, he went on.

Luckily for him, at the end of the tunnel, there was a door.

An elevator door.

He entered there and immediately pressed the button to close it.

The beast almost slammed into the closing doors.

His smile was the last thing he saw, mere inches away from the opening, as it closed.

He continued to press the button to close the door.

Accidentally, however, he also pressed another button.

One he could not remember.

At first, he did not notice it.

But then the lift started to move.

And it went upwards.

He panicked.

He almost started to cry.

He sure wanted to.

He thought about exiting the emergency lock on top of the elevator.

But he knew it would be dark outside.

And, potentially infested with smilers.

He decided to face what was on the other side of the door.

It was the right call.

As it started to open, John realized that there were no beasts waiting there for him.

It was similar to "level zero".
He went forward.
His knife was ready.
Although his first choice would always be to run away from any danger.
He slowly peeked from the corner.
What he saw, made him happy.
Another group of humans.
With faces.

One of them spotted John.
<< Hey there! >> she shouted.
Seeing that the woman was armed, he raised his arms as a sign of not being a dangerous being.
<< Don't shoot, I... I am human >>
She squared him down.
<< Yeah I know, what do you want? >>
<< I just came from an... an elevator, it was >> he stopped for a second.
Looking back, he saw no doors for the lift.
It was there seconds ago.
<< It was there, I think >>
<< Oh, a newbie >> she was visually becoming more relaxed, as she understood that John was potentially not a threat.
<< First time meeting people? >>
<< No, I've been to a diner on level one >>
<< Oh, Tom's one right? >>

He moved his face to confirm.

<< Sweet man, I was there weeks ago >>

<< So you are a "newbie" too? >>

<< Me? >> she laughed << No, I've been here for at least half a year >>

<< And what about your life before? I don't know, your family? Friends? Aren't they worried? >>

<< Relax man, time here moves differently. Most of those who can go back end up missing for only a brief amount of time, days, or even just hours if they are lucky. I once was here for an entire month and when I got back, only two days had passed >>

He moved closer.

<< Wait >> his voice was full of hope << You went back to the real world? >>

<< Yes, more than one time >>

<< And why... why you are still here? >>

<< Well, out there, in the front rooms, there are places more dangerous than some levels here. I, for example, was homeless before. The back rooms are now my home. We don't live in scarcity here, especially on the fourth level, this one. See that man over there? He's Jacob, he was a soldier in Iraq a couple of "real years" before. During an ambush, he was repositioning and no-clipped, ending up in level two. Trust me, don't go in there if you can, but I believe you already have been there. He's here now. At least, the risk of people shooting him is lower here. I'm Susan by the way >>

<< John >> he said, as he shook her hand.

<< That is also why some decide to remain here. Some don't have anything on the other side. Or no one. Some find this place comforting, and safe. Some simply surrendered. Others, even came here on purpose, to see if this place is real >>

<< Seriously? >>

<< Yeah, and those are almost always the unlucky ones. They know the place beforehand, yet the rooms have a weird sense of humor. Sometimes, the more you know, the more they throw at you >>

<< You mean monsters? >>

<< Yep >>

She introduced him to a couple of others there.

They were collecting resources for their group.

<< The M. E. G. ? >> I asked him.

<< Yes, Major Exploration Group. No, Explorer. Yeah, Major Explorer Group. M.E.G. >>

<< And I guess they do explore that place >>

<< Exactly >>

<< And what happened next? >>

<< She told me they were going to the city >>

The group finished packing up resources.
Mostly, almond water.
Then, they moved out.
While they were going around, they stopped to talk with a couple of other explorers.

With some, they exchanged goods.

It appeared a couple of them were already friends with the small group of the M.E.G.

With others, they simply exchanged pieces of information.

In one instance, the group did a U-turn to avoid another group.

They did not specify the reason why, yet John understood that the other group was potentially dangerous, as the members of his reached for their weapons and kept them ready until they were out of sight with the others.

Apparently, just like in the normal world, some people resort to violence to solve conflicts.

After what seemed a couple of hours, the group decided to rest in a big square.

It had another group inside, with whom they interacted.

There, they exchanged stories of their former selves.

Half of John's group went to sleep after eating some sandwiches.

He was in the half of the group that stayed awake.

He remained there with Susan and another man, simply called Tim.

No one knew his real name or surname.

Not even what he did before falling there.

At one time, as Tim went to take care of his biological business on the other side of a wall, Susan told John that she thought that Tim was one of those who wanted to stay there.

She was sure he was some kind of tax evader, or something down that line, who preferred to live in the back rooms rather than face the real world.

She also showed him a sort of a map.

It had a lot of blank spaces, and she taught him that the rooms continue to change.

There are, however, repeating patterns that can help you identify where you truly are.

And there are landmarks used by travelers to move between the levels.

If the objective was to simply travel from one level to another, they had to just connect the repeating patterns with the desired exit.

He tried to memorize various levels, the "most common ones", but it was too much info for his brain.

Then, they went to sleep.

He had been awake for probably days, yet he wasn't tired.

Still, he went.

To protect his sanity, the group suggested.

He followed their advice.

And dreamt of home.

CHAPTER IV: THE CITY

The group started moving again.
They exchanged a brief chat with the others and left.
As they were walking, they continued to exchange stories and, most importantly, bits of advice for John.
Getting lost was normal.
Therefore, they wanted to make sure that had he lost sight of them, he would still be able to survive out there, even if alone.
It was still better to move around in groups.
No doubt about that.
Jacob, who had the map, stopped everyone.
<< Okay, we're very close >>
<< Can you repeat me >> John asked Susan << where are we going? >>
<< First, we'll go through the Old Hotel, then we'll take a shortcut to the city >>
<< And is the city safe? >>
<< Yes, probably one of the safest places out there >>
<< And the Old Hotel? >>
<< Just follow us, trust me >>
The group restarted their walk.
After a couple of rooms, they found what they were looking for.
An old set of stairs.
They compacted the group.
They knew that those could disappear.

And that could leave some of the group behind.
They slowly walked in unison upwards.
The ceiling above was orange.
As they moved forward, the scenery became "older".
After some steps in the new environment, Susan
suggested that John looked back behind them.
The stairs had gone.
It reminded him of when he found the smiling beast.
He tried to forget about that being.

They traveled for a while.
John felt uneasy about that place.
It felt, haunted.
Especially the paintings on the walls.
He was sure some were following him with their eyes.
He wanted to tell Susan, but when he opened his mouth
to notify his fear, she nodded a yes before he could even
speak, and told him that he wasn't the only one with
that feeling.
She could almost read his mind now.
As they moved on, John started to hear something.
It was similar to a whisper.
He turned around.
No one was there.
Someone grabbed him by his shirt.
It was Jacob.
<< We need to move >>
They started to walk fast.

The whispers were getting near them.

From behind.

No living being was there.

Yet, the group soon started to run.

<< What was that? >> John asked.

They had been running for half an hour.

<< We don't know that yet >> replied Tim.

<< We're not the ones analyzing that thing, that's for sure >> followed Jacob.

They had told him that the M.E.G. had outposts on most of the levels.

In that one, there was a group of theirs called "House Keeping", whose job was to investigate how that level worked.

The M.E.G. wanted to transform that level into a safe one.

It wasn't that deadly.

At least, not most of it.

Some places were to be avoided at all costs.

While others were habitable.

The small group then started to hear Jazz music.

It was weird.

John was surprised.

And scared.

But the others weren't.

And that calmed him.

Quite the opposite, the group was almost happy about

that.

Susan told him that they were close to their objective, but first, he had to see something quite incredible.

And beautiful.

They traveled across a couple of smaller corridors.

The music was getting louder.

Then, they stopped in front of a door.

A small silver card labeled it.

John got closer to look at it.

"The Beverly Room".

They entered.

It was really beautiful.

It was a big ballroom.

In the middle of it, there was a table with a huge chandelier suspended above it, that illuminated most of the room.

In the walls, there were dozens of doors.

Some single, some double.

There were a lot of people in that portion of the Old Hotel.

As they moved forward, some people went toward them.

One of them had an old hotel staff suit and introduced himself as Max to John.

They shook hands.

Then Max went in front of Susan.

They both smiled and hugged each other.

<< John >> she turned towards him << this is my cousin, and he works here >>

<< So, new wanderer >> he asked John << Are you here by accident or by design? >>

<< Accident >>

<< I see >> he stopped for a second << but don't despair, I think you'll be able to find a way home >>

<< I really hope so >>

<< I'm sure Susan will be able to help you, right? >>
She confirmed.

Max started to explain to him what that place, that level, was.

As the group traveled across the room, John stopped for a second.

A young woman, with short hair, was talking to an old man in a tuxedo.

John's eyes however were attracted by a simple detail.

While she was dressed elegantly, like everyone else (except his own group), she was also wearing an aviator jacket over the dress.

<< That's Amelia >> Max told him with a low voice volume.

<< Wait... >>

<< Yes, that Amelia >>

<< Holy crap, are you serious? >>

<< I am. I would have told you to go towards her if only she did not hate talking to strangers >>

<< Why? >>

<< Do you think you are the first one who wants to speak with her? >>

   << Amelia Earhart? >> I asked him.
The patient replied affirmatively.
The more time it passed, the more I felt as if he had invented everything.
He had to.
That was the most logical conclusion.
He continued with his story.
They entered another room, that resembled the entry hallway of a hotel.
There, Max went towards the reception to search for a key.
When he came back, he hugged Susan again and told everyone goodbye as he opened the main door.
The group went across the exit, and found themselves in what John described as a "city of lights".
Artificial lights.
All around them.
Similar to a modern metropolis at night time.
They started running.
John was unable to see what danger they were running from.
They entered the second street and approached a door, the closest one.
They quickly crossed it.
And found themselves in another city.

This time, more normal.

They had just entered "level eleven".

The city they were seeking.

It looked normal.

<< Are we in the front rooms? >> asked John.

Susan smiled.

<< Sadly not, but this is one of the closest places to it
that you could find, at least in the lower levels >>

Apparently, the back rooms have tens of thousands of
levels.

Maybe even more.

Most, are unexplored.

This level, contrary to most other ones, had a lot of living
beings.

Human beings.

The group moved forward on the sidewalk of one of the
streets.

<< Morning Mr. and Miss. Tokyo >> Tim shouted.

An old couple, recognizable by the fact that they had
walking sticks with them and were very curved, turned
towards the group.

They were dressed in oriental clothes.

As soon as they faced the group, they bowed down, as a
gesture of salute, similarly to what Japanese people do.

But when they turned up again, John was terrified.

Facelings.

He wanted to scream, but Susan immediately

tranquilized him.

<< Don't worry, they are peaceful here >>

He looked at her in horror.

John then looked around.

He noticed that he was surrounded by facelings.

They were going by their day.

Truth is, most of the inhabitants of that city were facelings.

Most of them were impossible to tell apart from others.

Some, like the Tokyo couple, had weird clothes.

Those defined their name.

There was a young kid with his family.

A young faceling, of course.

While most of the time the kids are dangerous, he too was neutral here.

He wore a sports t-shirt with a big number one written on it.

His nickname was, of course, "number one".

When he got near the group, as they were moving along the street, Susan called him by that nickname, and he ran towards her to hug her.

The parents shook the hands of those in the group.

Including John.

Those beings, obviously, could not speak.

Some simply nodded.

Others used sign language.

They could hear, even if they had no ears.

They could see, even if they had no eyes.

But they lacked the capability to make any word.
Facelings.
Everywhere.
It took John some time to not be scared by that fact.

They reached their destination.
It was an office building near an old church.
There were a dozen or so other survivors there.
They all greeted John and the group there.
And the group spent the day there, taking a nap before going to the nearby park for a break.
Susan's husband, Harold, was there.
Harold was an ex-accountant from New York.
He had fallen into the backrooms in the early 2010s.
Susan saved him from a smiler.
And they fell in love.
Sometimes, they traveled together to the front rooms.
They hoped of being able to have a normal life out there.
Yet, sometimes they fell back to that place.
They had agreed that if one of the two was missing for three days in the normal world, they would find him or her there, in the city.
In the end, they decided to remain mostly in the backrooms.
They were going to have a wedding soon.
Their ones.
John tried to think about what it could have felt like to

raise a family there.
To live there, could be possible.
To work there, also.
But to have children, that was weird to him.
He couldn't imagine raising kids there.
Telling them that it was normal that some people had no face.
To tell them about the monsters.
Lie to them.
Or tell them the truth.
That they were bound to stay there forever.
In that parallel, dangerous universe.
He learned that children usually do not no-clip from the real world.
So, when he saw some, he immediately thought about the fact that they had been born here.
And that always gave him the chills.

     Time passed in the city.
Sometimes, he helped humans take care of the buildings.
There was an office floor in one structure that was being reconverted into a hotel.
John had no particular skill, yet he helped as much as he could.
After weeks, he even started to pass some time with facelings.
At first, it was hard.

But then it became natural.
They helped with the physical tasks in the construction.
There were various types of facelings that he met.
Construction workers.
Secretaries.
Office workers.
Accountants.
Lawyers.
Baristas.
Cleaners.
They performed all kinds of jobs.
They were like him.
Simply, with no face.
There was no night on that level.
Yet, there were still nighttime activities.
John went into some bars usually.
Sometimes, he got home drunk.
Inside his mind, he hoped to wake up in the normal world.
But every time, he was into the city.
The city of facelings, as he called it.
Others gave it the name of the endless city.
He believed that to be impossible.
Maybe it was just very big.
But not infinite.
Not endless.
One day he wanted to try and explore it all.
In the meantime, the hotel had been finished.

Therefore, they decided to throw a party to celebrate.
Both for humans and facelings.
They had, after all, equal rights there.
And they had contributed to the construction too.
So there was no motivation to leave them out.
And so, John went to the party.
He was used now to living in the city.
A month had passed.
Maybe more.
He was losing track of time.
Some told him that he had to lose that, as to avoid becoming worried about the outside world.
Others stated that time was the only thing keeping them sane, and he should always keep an eye on that.
He decided to follow the advice of the former.
Life was becoming easy.
Wake up.
Take a shower.
Dress up.
Go to work.
Get home.
And go to bed.
He usually ate at work and in his room.
Sometimes, he went out with some friends he made there, and ate outside, in bars or restaurants.
He also frequented discos and "night bars", which are pubs converted into giving those inside a feeling of nighttime.

The city had everything.
A couple of cinemas.
And the films had a combination of humans and
facelings.
Some looked like normal films of the outside world.
Others were about stuff he had never seen.
Tony, one of his friends, who was a New Yorker, was
convinced that facelings were real humans from another
dimension.
And that those facelings saw themselves as normal
humans, and them as facelings.
It was a weird theory.
But potentially plausible.
He had, obviously, no way to either confirm or deny that
theory.
He liked it.
It gave him a higher sense of "humanity" when he
encountered beings with no face.
Maybe, he hoped, that is why the facelings themselves
were so keen on helping everyone, with or without a
face.
It was similar to a utopia.
And he liked that place.

    He knotted his tie.
He was looking forward to this party.
A lot of people had been invited.
He would also see Susan again.

She had gone on some adventures and had returned two days before.

He hadn't been able to go to her house and greet her, yet he was sure she was alright.

Harold had told him.

John had started working under Susan's husband's watch as a junior accountant.

He was the owner of one of the many offices on the block.

Most of the employees were facelings.

John's direct boss was a faceling too.

He called him Kangaroo, as that man had a small pin on his suit, with a kangaroo drawn over him.

To differentiate himself from other humans, John wore a red tie and a fedora hat.

He was sure that, if Tony's theory was correct, the facelings could differentiate him from the others, and maybe they called him "red tie" or "funny hat".

In John's universe, the word "fun" had been basically banned.

There was apparently a level called like that.

With beings that would try and convince to "party with them".

It was a horrible tale.

John knew that, had he seen a balloon flying around for no apparent reason, he should move away from that area.

The balloons were dangerous.

Not by themselves.
But because of who, or what, controlled them.

John grabbed his fedora hat and fixed his jacket.
It was becoming slightly less cold, and he thought that
maybe winter was coming to an end.
While the city had no day and night cycle, maybe it had
seasons.
Yet, the trees still had leaves.
Maybe, they did not lose them.
Either way, that day, or should be called night, it was
colder than usual.
He exited the building, after waving at the faceling who
was at the reception.
He lived in a hotel, and although he hoped one day of
being able to return to his real home, he was starting to
lose hope.
So, he had started searching for an apartment.
And would soon be able to buy one.
Hopefully.
In the back rooms, there is not a "real" economy.
Most of the levels function on a simple barter logic.
If you have something that someone else wants, a deal
can be made.
Some levels however have so many people that it could
be possible to find a sort of representative money, as a
sort of promise of payment.
One of the levels with a sort of economic system is the

endless city one.

Various coins are exchanged by the wanderers there. The main three are the "Backdollar" (BKD), the "Commercidollar" (CMD) and the "Colo Dollar" (CLD). The first one was slowly getting replaced by the second one, and those are created and traded by the same group.

Still, there is also another currency, the "City Lira" (CYL) that was starting to circulate in relatively large numbers in level eleven.

John's salary was at first paid in CMDs, but had now recently been transferred to CYLs.

The exchange rate was very favorable, and that helped strengthen the city trade.

Not that it needed it.

The endless city was a very popular destination, with millions of inhabitants (mainly facelings) and with a booming economy.

No buildings were being built, but the insides were continuously renovated.

John knew that the CYLs were having inflation and deflation problems, but since he wasn't an expert in finance, he didn't care.

All he cared is that what once would have given him one gallon of almond water, now he would be able to buy five gallons.

Harold was also involved in the "push" for the new currency in the city.

There were factions that accused the city inhabitants of risking an economic crash.

It was funny.

They were trapped God knows were, and they cared about money.

The worst to understand were the facelings however.

Simply because they couldn't speak.

They could gesticulate.

Others were able to write.

Tony supposed that those unable to write in English were ex-inhabitants of non-English speaking countries.

Plausible.

That would also explain why some dressed in weird foreign clothing, at least to John's eyes.

He entered the bar.

It was on Avenue 67, on the parallel street to where John lived.

It was very crowded, and the music was terribly loud.

He was able to spot in the distance Harold, and he approached his superior.

They greeted each other.

As they started talking, someone tapped on John's shoulders.

When he turned, he saw Susan.

She was well.

The expedition had been a success, and she would soon depart on another one.

After that, she had promised him that they could try to bring John to the front rooms.

Harold was against the idea.

Not only because John was an invaluable worker for his firm.

Mainly, because he was sure that one day he would fall back down.

He reasoned that, once the backrooms "take" you once, they will forever take you again.

It becomes an inescapable prison.

Still, his wife wanted to try.

She wanted John to remain too, but she knew that forcing someone on remaining somewhere was bad.

John was introduced to another couple.

The first one to enter the backroom of the two was the girl, who then convinced the husband to move there with her.

It seemed to John that as more time passed, the population of the backrooms was increasing.

Maybe it was because the general population in the "real" Earth was booming.

Yet, this place was real too.

At least to him.

And he had started noticing more and more children around.

Obviously, not only humans.

Facelings too.

There were also some mixed couples.

One human and one faceling.

He was intrigued by the idea, but also thought it to be very strange to fall in love with someone whose face you can't see.

He would surely have preferred a human companion.

At the same time, he didn't.

Inside him, he wanted to escape.

Escape from there.

Go away.

And never return.

To wake up from what was possibly his most complex dream.

Or, better described, his most complex nightmare.

He had visited some parts of the backrooms.

Always with someone else.

With Tony, to be more precise, they had visited the field of wheat (known as "level 10").

They also visited The Hub.

In those two levels, they usually stocked up on supplies.

To arrive at The Hub, they used The Metro.

Some define it as a level in itself, while others indicate it as simply a connection between zones.

He had been advised to always be careful with The Metro or other transportation systems, as those could lead to very dangerous places.

One day they had accidentally missed the city stop while returning and ended up in level 36, an almost empty airport terminal.

Luckily, it was a safe place.

Yet, John still had a curiosity about some of the levels.

Some he had simply heard of.

From others, he had also seen pictures and sometimes even some videos.

It seemed as if every new wanderer had a new story.

They all shared the first levels.

Then, depending on what each and every one of them did, different paths were taken that eventually led them to the endless city.

He had also found out that facelings as well do travel.

However, on some levels they are peaceful.

In others, they are not.

Due to this, when he used The Metro he always traveled in the "human only" carts.

The carts were similar to everyone else.

They were just inhabited by humans only.

Facelings too tended to "segregate themselves" indifferent carts.

The reason is unknown.

The music stopped for a second, and one of the DJs thanked everyone there for coming by, before putting on other music.

John started dancing.

He was happy that day.

His friend Susan was back.

He had worked hard, yet he had achieved a lot in the last

24 hours.
He tried to not think about work.
Not at that moment.
He had to have some fun.
He deserved it.
So he danced.

He was enjoying the "night".
He had drunk a lot in the last hours.
Then, accidentally, he bumped into a person.
As he tried to help that human, he realized that she wasn't a person.
She was a faceling.
Yet, something had caught his eye.
She wore a red pin on her dress.
He had already seen it.
She worked with him!
Not in the same office.
But in the same building.
They had, in the past, exchanged looks at each other.
At least, John had looked at her multiple times.
She had no eyes.
Yet he was sure that, whenever she encountered him, she would look at him.
She fixed her hair and waved at him.
They were awkwardly close, and the salute was even weirder.
He excused himself.

He then realized that she probably couldn't hear him, as it was very loud.

So, he took out a small notebook.

Taking a note, he wrote down his excuses.

She took the piece of paper and nodded.

John was sure that, even if she had no face, it was as if she had smiled at him.

Maybe it was the movement of the head.

Maybe the body position.

She replied on the note that it wasn't a problem and that her name was Alissa.

He wrote down his name.

He was curious about her.

Suddenly, she started writing down something.

She asked him if they could go briefly outside, as she had a question for him.

He hesitated a little.

Even if they were in level 11, she was still a faceling.

On that level, almost all facelings were peaceful.

Some were, however, not.

There had been some murders.

Facelings on humans.

Humans on humans.

Facelings on facelings.

It was normal.

He agreed with his head.

She took his arm and navigated their way outside.

Her hand was as cold as ice.

Before he was able to turn around and notify his friends, he found himself outside.
Alone with her.
Some people were exiting the bar.
Others, entering.
They sat down on a short concrete wall.
She started writing.
She had a very decisive writing technique.

Sorry if I have been so brute, I've just seen you at work and I wanted to know more info on "you".

He raised his shoulders, unable to understand what she wanted to know.
She continued:

I just want to know how your life is, how do you do everyday activities and other stuff.

He grabbed the pencil.

What do you want to know about me?

Everything.

May I ask you a question first? It's somewhat rude to answer a question with another question, yet those similar to me have not been able to answer this to me, and I really want to know this.

What do you want to know?

How do you see me?

When she took the note, she kept it in her hands.
She moved her head towards him.
She seemed surprised.

Can I draw it?

Sure

Close your eyes for a moment, please. Open them when I tap your chest.

He closed his eyes.
He was able to hear her hand drawing down something on his note.
That was something that Tony had wanted to know for a long time.
How do facelings see us, humans?
John remained like that for a while.
Then the writing sound stopped.
After a couple of seconds, she tapped his chest.
He opened his eyes.
He looked at her.

Then looked at the note she was offering him.
She had written:

I hope this drawing does not offend your people.

He turned the page around.
And screamed.

<< Wait, let me understand >> I stopped him for a second.
<< You mean that she drew a faceless face? >>
<< Exactly >>
<< But you do have a face >>
<< And so do they, it's just that we cannot see theirs, and they can't see ours >>
<< So there are more than one "type" of human >>
<< It appears so >>
I was shocked.
That was the weirdest "story" a patient had ever told me.
He continued.
As they sat there, they exchanged information about their respective people.
It turned out, that they were very similar.
Eerily similar.
He felt tired.
The excitement and terror about that news had now vanished.

Now, he simply was tired.

She was too.

Yet, as they both wanted to know more about each other's "people", they planned on meeting again in the following days.

She invited him to where she lived, a part of the city that was reachable with The Metro, a couple of stations before it would take the passengers to the empty airport.

He agreed to that proposal.

As he went home, he was intrigued.

His friends had mixed feelings about the situation.

Susan was happy for him.

Although he knew that she had potentially misinterpreted what he wanted to tell her.

Maybe she understood that he had been invited to a "date" with the faceling.

It was simply an encounter to learn more about the other person.

In concept, it was similar to a date.

There, you meet someone and try to understand them to see if they could become a potential partner for you.

This was not with the intent of becoming potential partners.

At least, that is what he understood.

It was simple curiosity between the two.

Harold was against that meeting.

Despite being a person who was surrounded by

facelings, he still was suspicious of them.

He was always on alert when those were around him.

Not that he could be blamed.

Even in level 11, facelings should not be "threatened".

What accounted as a threat, however, depended on the faceling itself.

Some were angered by even looking at them.

Others could even be punched and would not answer violently.

They were an interesting species.

Tony was enthusiastic about the idea.

He and John had met the following day for breakfast.

At first, he wanted to ask if he could come too, yet it quickly became apparent that it would be a bad idea.

The main problem is that Alissa could have felt "endangered" and could have become aggressive if she found some unplanned guest in her house.

They thought about telling her beforehand, yet they quickly realized it was unfeasible.

She didn't give John her phone number.

And, mainly, she was a faceling.

She had no way to speak, as she had no mouth!

A letter would take too much time to arrive.

Surely it would have arrived after they had planned their meeting.

The best course of action was therefore to simply ask her (with a note, as all the conversations with facelings were) if the next time Tony could come too.

<< Maybe she has a faceling friend for me >> joked him.

John looked surprised at his friend.

<< I've always known you're a creep, but damn, this is new to me >>

<< Hey, it was a joke >>

<< Yeah... sure >>

He wasn't convinced.

His friend's interest in that other species was... weird.

Almost obsessive.

Maybe, John thought, he was a stalker or a "mixer".

He pushed those ideas aside.

His friend was just lonely.

He was too.

But he wasn't too desperate.

Surely not with a faceling.

He remembered a dream he had on one of the first nights in the city.

He was on the shore of a lake.

A girl was beside him, and they were looking at the sun coming down.

He, subconsciously, felt at home.

In the real one.

In the front rooms.

As his brain was relaxing, his dream become soon a nightmare.

The girl turned her head and faced him.

She had the same hair as the woman on level 1.

She got closer to his face.

He, scared, got up.

As she did the same, he pushed her away.

She fell down the small hill and ended up in the water.

As she got up, soaking wet, she become to shake.

Facelings sometimes do that.

Most of the time, it is a bad sign.

A sign of danger.

He started walking uphill, backward.

She was starting to gain ground, so he turned and was almost ready to start running when he bumped into another faceling.

He fell to the ground.

Looking up, he saw more and more facelings.

Surrounding him.

Touching him.

His head.

As if they wanted to steal it.

He then woke up, soaking wet in sweat.

His heart was pumping fast.

As if it wanted to run out of his body.

He almost had a heart attack.

He reached for his almond water bottle and drank it entirely.

He then went to the bathroom as his body was full of water.

It was almost his time to go to the office for one of his first days, so he decided to stay up and not try to go back to bed.

It would have been useless anyway.

He did his business in the bathroom, and when he flushed down the toilet he was sure he had heard laughs behind him.

With his pants still down, he turned his head to face a potential threat.

It wasn't there.

The door was closed.

He started dressing up.

He put on his suit trousers and a white t-shirt.

All gifted by Harold.

He then proceeded to wash his face.

With almond water.

He then rubbed the wetness away with a towel.

When he looked at himself in the mirror, however, he almost fell over.

His face was gone.

He panicked and rubbed his eyes.

His face was still there when he opened them.

He relaxed a little.

Having finished his morning routine, he then opened the bathroom door.

He looked at his bed, on which he saw a female faceling laying there, "looking" at him.

He ran towards the door.

He entered the corridor of the hotel, and on one end of it, he saw a faceling.

Not that it was uncommon.

It was, after all, the endless city.

And that faceling wasn't a threat.

Yet, he felt it as such, so he ran away in the opposite direction.

He knew that running was forbidden.

Not only because the noise could annoy someone in the various rooms.

The main risk was no-clipping.

He did not care.

He thought the room was haunted.

He preferred to no-clip and end up who knows where, rather than seeing another damn faceling.

He slammed his fist against a door that he knew was of the room of a human being.

She opened the door.

He jumped inside and slammed the door behind him.

She stood there, looking at him surprised.

He explained what had happened.

And she tried to ease him, calm him down, telling him that it was normal.

Facelings' nightmares are normal.

Mainly because they look so similar to us.

Especially in that level.

He still was too scared.

And after that, he decided to move out of that apartment.

He went in a building with more humans inside.

There, he felt safer.

He was brought back to reality by Tony.

He had grabbed his hand and stopped it.

The reason was that he had been mixing the sugar in his coffee for at least fifteen minutes.

After that nightmare, he never stayed alone with a faceling.

Until he had met Alissa.

He felt safe with her.

Even knowing quite well how he could end up if she got mad at him for whatever reason.

If she did, God save him.

He would have ended up in one of those articles that Harold was used to reading.

If he would have even been found at all.

CHAPTER V: THE TRIP

The days passed.

He had accidentally encountered Alissa a couple of times in the buildings where he worked at.

Every time, it was awkward.

It did not help the fact that someone had started a rumor that they were seeing each other.

It was, weird.

Very weird.

He didn't know who could have started that rumor.

Susan? Improbable, as she had departed for another expedition the day after she knew that.

Harold? Maybe he wanted someone else, possibly his colleagues, to try and convince him to not go.

He was, after all, scared of losing his employee.

And John as well knew that he was playing with fire.

Tony? Maybe he had been "jealous" that it wasn't him with a faceling.

He couldn't understand where it came from.

It made him a little embarrassed.

He knew that people were looking at him.

Humans.

And facelings.

He felt as if all the city's eyes were on him.

He wanted to sink down, under the pavement.

He wanted to hide.

A couple of times, he thought about telling Alissa that he

was booked on the day planned.

Or whatever.

He would have been able to find an excuse.

Yet, he did not cancel.

He was embarrassed when he was with her.

The fact that they had to "speak" with signs and letters was contributing to the embarrassment.

He also found himself struggling to work, especially with facelings.

He was always thinking about Alissa.

And not always in a good sense.

Luckily, the endless city is one of the few levels that could be mapped with some kind of accuracy, at least most of it.

Therefore, he was able to buy a map of the city.

And he was lucky to find that the address that she gave him was visible on the map.

He studied it.

Every way in.

And every way out.

Each potential escape route.

He was scared.

Intrigued also.

But mainly scared.

What he didn't know, was if he was scared of doing something wrong that could offend her culture and make her less interested in him, or if he was scared of accidentally doing something that she could perceive as dangerous and making himself a potential target for an attack.

Either way, he wasn't keen on doing either of those.

He thought about bringing her flowers, but that was not only embarrassing but also disrespectful.

She had no nose, after all.

Then, the day arrived.

He started his morning as usual.

It was a Saturday, so that day he wasn't working.

He woke up early, as to spend more time preparing himself.

After taking a long shower (with almond water), he took some time to do morning skincare.

He then picked his outfit.

At first, he had decided to wear a suit.

But then opted for a more informal polo instead of a shirt underneath.

Plus, that day was weirdly hot.

So the outfit was matching the outside temperature and seem normal out there.

He exited his room and took the stairs.

He had been advised to not take the elevators in that level, as those could bring him elsewhere.

Imagine having planned to meet a neutral faceling, and ending up in level two instead.

Maybe the smiler was still there where he left it months prior, near the elevator doors.

He shrugged that idea off from his mind.

That night, he had dreamt of Alissa.

He dreamt of walking with her in a neighborhood at night.

They were going only under the various light poles, when suddenly in the distance they had started to turn off.

One after another.

They then ran away from the turning off lights.

Not only because of undefined creatures nearby but also because she had told him that facelings get more aggressive at night, even in level 11.

Yes, she told him.

She spoke.

He couldn't see her, yet he was sure that it was her voice.

Despite having never heard it.

He was sure of it.

Then, still in his dream, they had no clipped and ended up in a pool.

No one else was around.

They walked for a mile or so until they had ended up in a hotel hall.

There, they chatted.

He heard, again, her voice.

It was, natural.

Similar to a human voice.

He was sure that, under that unseeable veil that seemed

to cover her face, she was human.
There were legends of humans becoming facelings.
He was, obviously, scared of that.
Maybe by transforming he would be able to see her.
Maybe she was bringing him to her house to do that.
To transform him.
He hoped not.
While he was intrigued by her, he still wanted to remain human.
Not become a faceling.
He forgot how the dream ended.
One second, she was talking normally.
The next one, she was mumbling incoherently and then her voice became similar to his own wake-up alarm.
It was his wake-up alarm.
He felt a little melancholy as he woke from the bed.
But now that feeling had passed.
He was happy of being able to meet her.
He walked fast down the road.
Almost going against a couple of facelings and humans who were unlucky enough of working on a Saturday morning.
He walked down the stairs of The Metro station nearby.
He bought no ticket, as those aren't needed in the backrooms.
Trains come and go every day.
No tickets are required.
The only thing checked is what type of being you are.

Humans, facelings, and hounds.
Hounds are four-legged monsters that are highly
dangerous in levels other than the "safe" ones, such as
level 11.
They are extremely creepy as well.
Luckily, carts are separated.
He boarded the train that was on the platform.
He risked losing it but was able to catch it on time.
He found himself surrounded by facelings, and so he had
to move, as the train departed, into the next wagon.
He sat down.
And started counting the stations.
Nine stations to go.
After a couple of them, however, he fell asleep.

He dreamt of his home.
His real home.
His apartment in the outskirts of Chicago.
In his dream, he had just gone home, and he had found
it abandoned.
As if he had been away for a decade.
It was a horrible sight.
As he was looking around for something salvageable, he
heard a noise.
He went to check and, with horror, realized that there
was a smiler there.
That being looked at him.
Then, he jumped towards him.

He suddenly woke up.
He wasn't home.
There were no smilers nearby.
He was still in the backrooms.
Still on the train.
He looked outside the window.
With horror, he realized that he had overslept.
He was at the abandoned airport station.
He quickly got up, moving towards the train door.
He was almost outside when they closed.
He frantically searched for the manual opening lever.
He couldn't find it.
As the train accelerated, his panic grew.
He tried searching again but was unable to find the
lever.
He had no idea where the train was leading him.
Where it would bring him.
He knew that some levels were safe, and others
dangerous.
Which ones were which, that he couldn't tell.
He tried remembering the train line map.
Nothing.
He was scared.
From head to toe.
He sat back down.
And then he got up again.
Looking around the cart, he searched for a map.
Nothing.

He heard a noise.
It was coming from another wagon.
He looked over and saw some facelings looking at him.
He understood that the train was leaving the Endless City.
It was leaving a safe area.
Facelings could soon become dangerous.
He hoped that, by not making any sudden movement or loud sounds, he could be seen as passive.
He sat down, again.
This time, keeping the corner of his eyes towards the beings with no face.
He glazed across the window.
Outside, it was dark.
Night.
They were traveling across an empty field.
He tried to find some known objects outside, some famous buildings.
Nothing.
He searched for any light.
Also nothing.
It was as if he was going into complete darkness.
The only thing lit out there was the train itself.
And the shadow of light casted by the window of the train.
The facelings were still standing near the cart door.
And still looking at him.
He then realized he was the only human there.

He tried to think as to why no one had awakened him.
He then realized that the last humans had probably left at the last city station, and thought that he was going to the airport.
He suddenly thought about Alissa.
He felt terrible.
He would be late.
If, he would be able to arrive at all.
The train started to slow down.
At first, he could simply hear the whistle made by the brakes.
Then, he felt the train starting to decelerate.
Outside, they weren't anymore in the middle of nothing.
They were in a suburban area.
Weird lights were in the middle of the streets.
The train came to a stop.
John watched the facelings exit the vehicle.
He hoped that he would be able to remain inside, as maybe the train would go back to a safer place.
Sadly for him, his hope was dashed by the metallic voice that informed the passengers that this was the end station and that all passengers had to exit.
The "all" felt to him particularly hostile.
Especially towards him.
Therefore, he grabbed what little courage he could master and timidly exited the train.
The train station was dark.
And that was a good thing.

He wanted to avoid the light.

He took the stairs that led him down to one of the main streets.

No creatures were in sight.

After looking around, and seeing no humans, he decided to remain near the station.

Maybe he would be able to board the train again and go back to where he came from.

But when he turned back, the train was not there anymore.

It was… gone.

Vanished.

That wasn't a good sign.

He started moving forward.

At first, slowly.

Then, he took up his pace.

He felt similarly scared to when he had first entered level zero.

He had lived for a long time now in the apparent safety of the city.

Out here, in the suburbs, he felt vulnerable.

As if his instincts had been buried.

And he now needed to find them again.

Fastly.

As his survival depended on that.

He walked on the sideway.

The street was emanating a sort of very low fog.

It was actually hot around there, despite being night.
It looked as if the pavement of the street had just been laid.
And it looked fresh.
And unsecure.
He did not want to test his theory.
He went forward.

He roamed for around an hour.
Remaining near the train station.
He hoped of finding a train back.
But every time he looked at the station, it was still empty.
He also started encountering creatures.
He was lucky that none were able to see him.
Mostly, those beings were facelings.
He felt like when in zombie movies the characters need to adapt to the fact that people they earlier shared spaces were now dangerous.
It was a similar situation.
He had to fight his urge to go outside and ask them for help.
As he knew that, out there, alone, in the dark, he was easy prey.
He also spotted a couple of hounds in the distance.
Yet, he wasn't ready yet for one of the worst beasts he had ever seen.
No one had prepared him for that.

He was ready to cross a path when his eyes were
suddenly caught by something moving nearby.
He hid behind a bush.
That thing got near him.
It was a giant floating eye.
<< A what? >> I asked him.
<< A giant eye, you know, the bulb of the eye >>
I continued writing down what he was telling me.
I was sure he was in some sort of deep psychosis or he
had done the biggest drug trip I had ever heard of.
The eye got near him.
It was mere feet away.
And it was scanning the street.
It remained there for some minutes.
Then it turned.
Towards him.
He was sure that he was a dead man.
But that thing did not see him.
Or, if it did, it decided not to attack him.
As it moved on.
Away from him.
He stayed there for another entire minute.
Then, having realized that his safest bet would probably
be to go inside a building, he moved out towards the
entrance of one.
The wooden stairs made a horrible sound.
The door, even worse.
But the inside seemed comfortable.

It was similar to a normal home.

Slowly checking the insides, he found no sign of other beings there.

The only weird feature was that the sofa and the table were almost fused together.

Melted together.

He looked outside a window.

Outside, there was a forest.

A door led from the sitting room to the outside.

He decided that he wouldn't go there.

So, he turned towards the door from which he came.

As he was about to turn the handle, a smiler appeared suddenly from the window nearby.

John panicked and, without thinking twice, moved in the opposite direction.

An inhuman screech cracked through the silence.

He wasn't sure if the smiler caused it, or another being.

What he was sure of, was that he wouldn't stay there to know the answer.

He opened the door and started running towards the forest.

He knew that in most levels if you go far enough you may end up in another level.

He hoped to find the wheatfield.

That was a safe zone.

So, he ran as fast as he could.

As he was going forward, he looked behind him.

The smiler had climbed over the roof of the house and

had just jumped down from it.
Running towards him.
Inside his mind, he prayed.
And he ran.
Something caught his attention, as he was running.
Something blue was flying above.
It was a bird.
While he looked at it, he got distracted by a fraction of a
second.
And he did not notice a branch that was in his path.
At least, not until he fell on it.

He hit his head.
But he did not blacked out.
The dirt was cold.
And wet.
He immediately got up and continued running.
He looked behind himself and he could bet that a light
was coming toward him.
The smiler was gaining ground.
He approached what looked like an opening.
He was on top of a hill.
Forward.
Down the slope.
He tripped a couple of times.
Yet, he still went forward.
On the valley between that hill and the next one, in the
middle of the trees, he saw what looked like a street.

As he reached, he quickly decided to go left, along the road.
He continued running.
He heard the screech again.
He had no idea where he was.
All he knew, was that if he wanted to live, he had to run.
The road was not straight.
Quite the opposite.
As he was running, sometimes he checked behind himself.
Looking for the smiler.
He couldn't see it.
But John was sure that those monsters were clever.
And they loved to ambush wanderers.
What he failed to notice were the lights coming in front of him.
On the street.
He saw them as he caught the light beam creating a shadow behind him.
He turned around, and the lights almost caught him.

He stopped completely still on the road.
He tought he was dead.
But he was lucky.
It wasn't a group of smilers.
It was something else.
Something way better.
Those lights, were from a car.

The vehicle stopped mere inches from him.

He almost got run over.

He pounded on the car hood while pointing behind him.

Screaming to those inside the old Mercedes to go back.

The car stood still.

Those inside it were looking terrified at him.

John looked at them and wasn't able to see any face.

He realized that, maybe, he was in level 69.

That could explain the car.

Not the facelings.

Not that he cared, however.

He started running again.

The road went downward, so he picked up speed as he went forward.

John was starting to feel exhausted.

He continued to look back.

The car had turned around.

Maybe it was dangerous too.

Damned facelings.

They had brought him outside of the city.

So that they could kill him.

He felt his energies deplete.

His feet were stopping.

He almost tripped over a couple of times.

Yet he had to go forward.

But the car was too close.

He quickly decided to stop and make a stand.

Maybe he would also be able to steal the car.

He turned towards the vehicle, that had just stopped.
John saw the facelings come out of it.
As he tried to reach for his knife, he found his eyes losing sight.
Then, something painful.
Behind his head.
He looked up.
He saw the top of the trees, stretching upwards.
A light rain was coming down.
Some drops hit his eyes.
His knife wasn't there anymore.
He started crying.
Then, John noticed the facelings.
They were getting near him.
Around him.
Like in his nightmares.
Maybe, he thought, he was a dead man.
From the instant, he had entered the backrooms.
He just wasn't brave enough to acknowledge it.
That was his last thought before he passed out.

CHAPTER VI: WHAT A STORY

I looked at the time.

Sadly, his appointment was finished.

He had simply the time to tell me that the next thing he remembered was being in a hospital.

No one knew what he was mumbling about.

Levels.

Facelings.

M.E.G.

Smilers.

Hounds.

No one understood.

They sedated him many times to keep him calm.

And, when he got better, he was analyzed by a psychologist.

They thought he was crazy.

Mentally ill.

He had, after all, been found with only a polo on himself during wintertime.

Yet, that man looked to him similar to Harold.

And he refused to explain in an understandable way to the doctor what had happened.

He was then released to the streets and found himself in Raleigh, North Carolina.

He tried to understand what level it was.

It took him a while to understand that he wasn't in the back rooms anymore.

He was home.
Distant from his physical home, in Chicago.
But still on the same "level", the front rooms.
It took him a while to also get back to Chicago.
And when he asked for a good psychologist, he searched for me.
That was because I am specialized in mental illnesses.
And in cases of severe PTSD.
And he surely looked like one.
He couldn't sleep at night.
He was scared of going around alone.
He walked weirdly, trying to avoid no-clipping.
Whatever happened to him, he still had the scars of that adventure on himself.

He missed the third appointment.
He invented an excuse, saying that he had found a job.
It wasn't the first time I had heard a patient saying something similar.
I started to think about what had I done wrong.
I usually was able to convince patients to remain for a lot of sessions.
I was looking forward to the third one.
In the first two, I simply listened.
For the next one, I hoped of solving some questions that had arisen in me.
But he did not come.
Not the third time, and not the fourth.

Every time, he delayed with more and more time between each appointment.
Every time, with a more extreme excuse.
I was starting to feel that I was losing him.
I was almost ready to call the cops one time.
I was worried.
That day, my studio wasn't the one making the call.
He had called me.
He booked an appointment for the following day.
I was relieved.

But, when the day came, he did not show up.
Nor he answered the phone.
Maybe he was late.
Maybe, he was still driving.
Night came.
Nothing.
I decided to call the cops the following day.
They went to his home, but he wasn't there.
It was as if he had quickly packed his stuff around and left.
To where no one knew.
I felt for the worst.
Maybe he had taken his own life.
That made me sad.
Every day, countless people who are not neurotypical die.
Most of them, do by suicide.

And the sad thing is that most of them could be stopped.
The reason is a lot of the time the stigma that society
has against them.
The other main reason is that sometimes they cannot,
sadly, control their demons anymore.
A city-wide search was initiated.
Sniff dogs were unable to trace his odor.
They simply pointed at a wall.
I started suspecting an idea.

Then, one day, a small box arrived at my office.
I opened that.
It contained a handwritten letter:

Dear Doctor (I forgot your name).
I don't know when this package will arrive.
If I am not still here, don't come to search me.
I have decided to go.
To where, you know it.
You will not believe me.
I wanted to go back.
I knew that I had left something back.
Maybe, my sanity.
Maybe, don't know.
I know you have not believed me and my story.
I would like to invite you here, but I don't want to kill
your mind too.
I had to go back.

Sorry if you feel sad.
John M.

I fell on my chair.
He had really decided to go back.
My guts proved me right.

But the box had also something else inside.
Not only the letter.
There was a piece of furniture.
It was wet.
Old.
The color, was piss yellow.
It took my breath away.
I looked at the other thing inside.
A small portable dashcam.
Another letter.

You will not believe my story, but I hope you believe your
own eyes. I had, during all the time, my service dashcam
on my belt. It recorded everything.
I hope it still works.

It worked.
I saw it.
I saw them.
Everything.
The backrooms.

All that he had told me.

I was a non-believer, then I saw.

And I now believe.

I do believe they exist.

And, if they really do, pray that you are lucky enough to never fall there.

I sure pray to remain in the front doors.

I decided to ask a person I know to write this story down.

To tell the tale of John.

That name is, obviously, invented.

I still want to protect his identity.

That explains why I asked to indicate this book as a work of fiction.

His story, on the other hand, is real.

The backrooms.

They are real.

Made in United States
Troutdale, OR
06/28/2023

10849567R00064